The Everything Seed

A Story of Beginnings

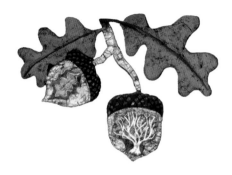

With hope and joy,
I lovingly dedicate this story to my grandchildren,
Asher Dominic and Olivia Clara,
and to the child spirit within each of us.

—Carole Martignacco

Text copyright © 2006 by Carole Martignacco
Illustrations copyright © 2006 by Joy Troyer

Tricycle Press
a little division of Ten Speed Press
P.O. Box 7123
Berkeley, California 94707
www.triclepress.com

Interior design by Chloe Rawlins, based on an original design by Joy Troyer
Cover design by Cassandra Lynn Young
Typeset in Baker Signet, Fontesque, Gill Sans, and Myriad
The illustrations in this book were rendered in batik on fabric.

Library of Congress Catalog Number: 2003105448
ISBN 13: 978-1-58246-161-8
ISBN 10: 1-58246-161-9

First Tricycle Press printing, 2006
Printed in China

1 2 3 4 5 6 — 09 08 07 06

The Everything Seed

A Story of Beginnings

by Carole Martignacco
Illustrated by Joy Troyer

TRICYCLE PRESS
Berkeley | Toronto

Have you ever watched
a seed grow?

Have you ever noticed
how it begins
so small,
so still,
so quiet,
like a gift wanting to be opened…

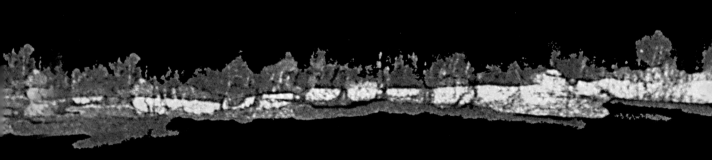

and how slowly
it wakes up,
begins to unfold,
growing
into something
larger…

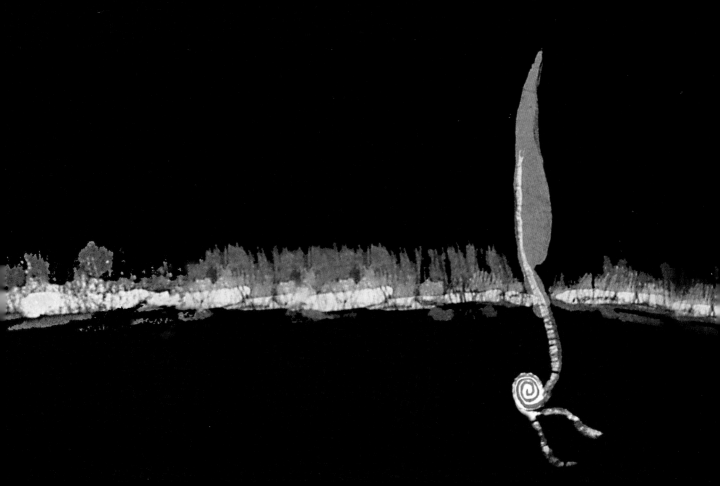

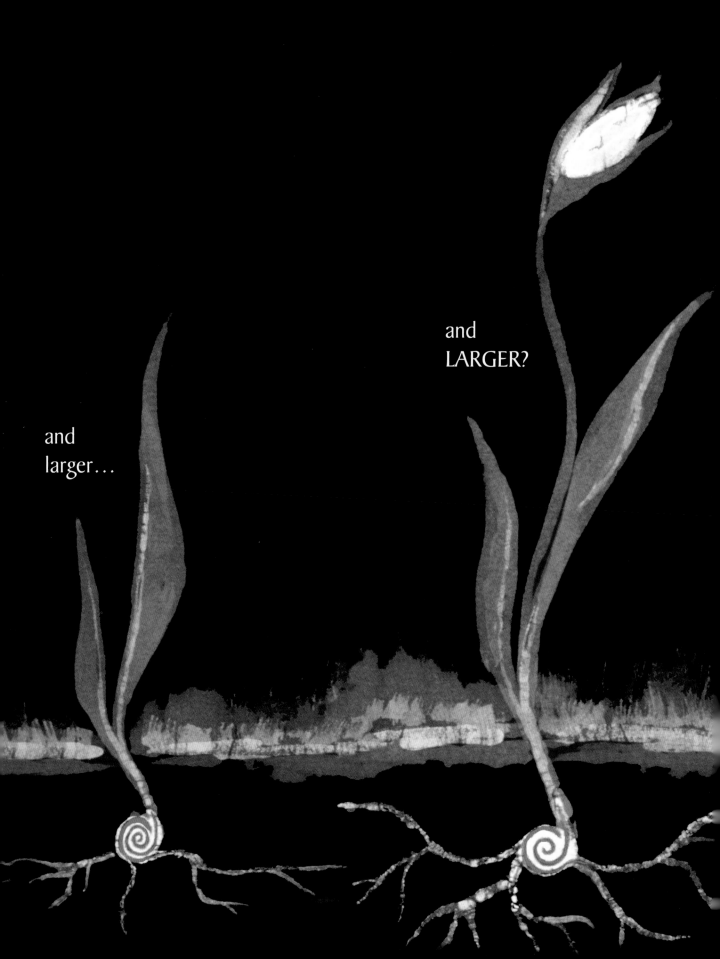

and
larger…

and
LARGER?

Then you know
that whatever
comes from a seed
usually ends up
looking very little like
the seed it came from…

which is also true
of the very first
seed.

Once, long, long ago,
way back before the beginning…
    so long ago
    there was no such thing
    as time, because
    there was no one there
    to count it…
Everywhere was
a huge
deep
mysterious
place,
like something
waiting to happen.

There were no stars,
no Sun or Moon.
There was no place like Earth…
    not a drop of water,
    or a single tree,
    or rock,
    or flower…
and no living beings anywhere.

But in that deep
waiting space
was hidden
the tiniest point
of something
no bigger than
a seed.

It was not
    a flower seed.
    It was not an oak tree seed.
    It was not a seed of corn,
    although all those things
    were included in the seed.

You might call it
an Everything Seed
because that
is what it became.

No one knows where that first seed came from,
or how it was planted,
or how it knew (in the way that only
seeds seem to know) how long to wait
for just the right moment
to sprout and grow.

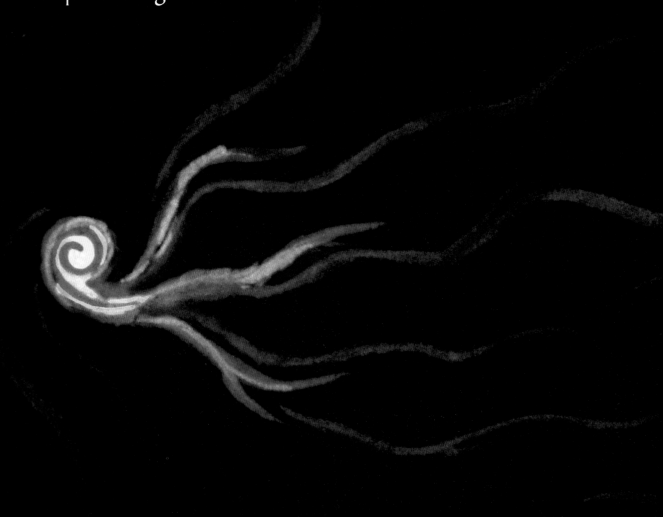

But all at once, this tiny seed,
cradled and nourished
in the rich soil of space,
woke up,
broke open,
and began
to unfold.
Unfolding…

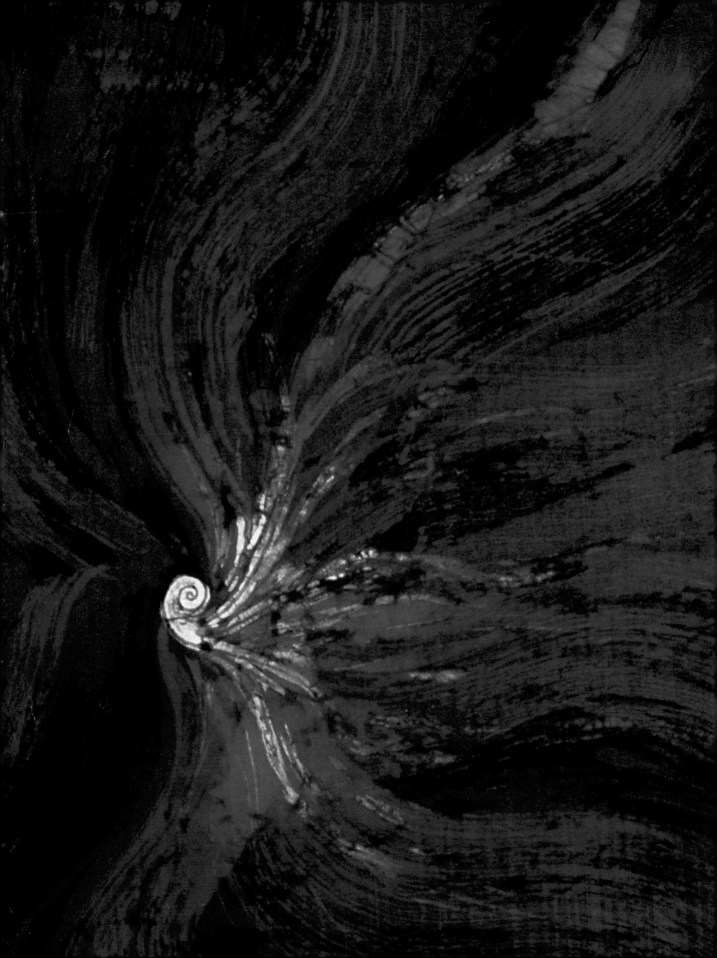

Unfolding…

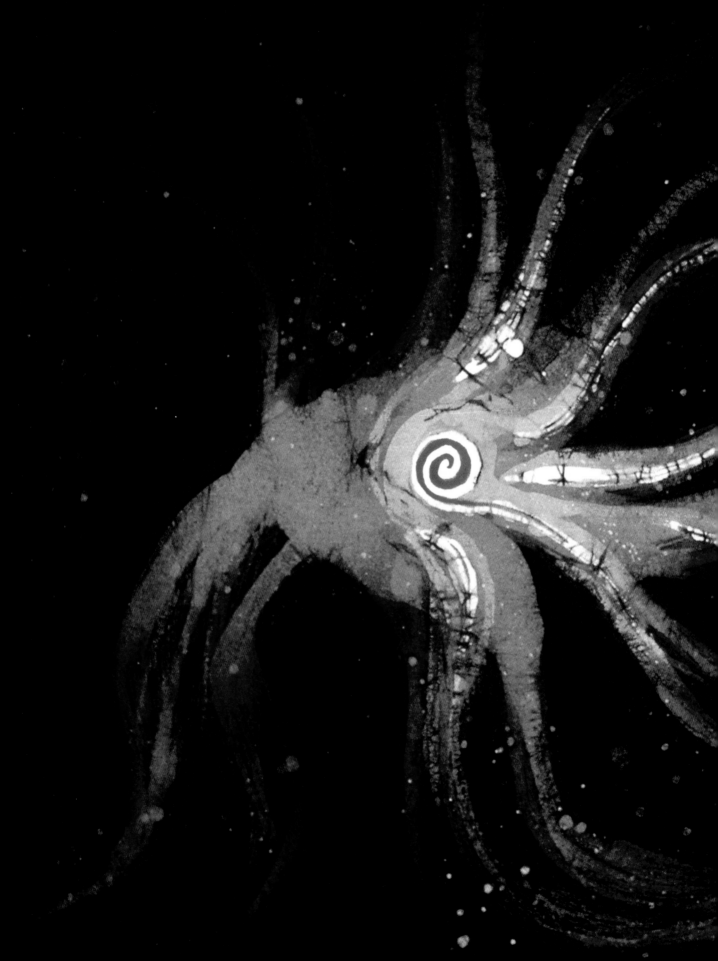

and blossoming forth…

into an enormous blazing
ball of bright light…

like a great
Grandmother Sun.

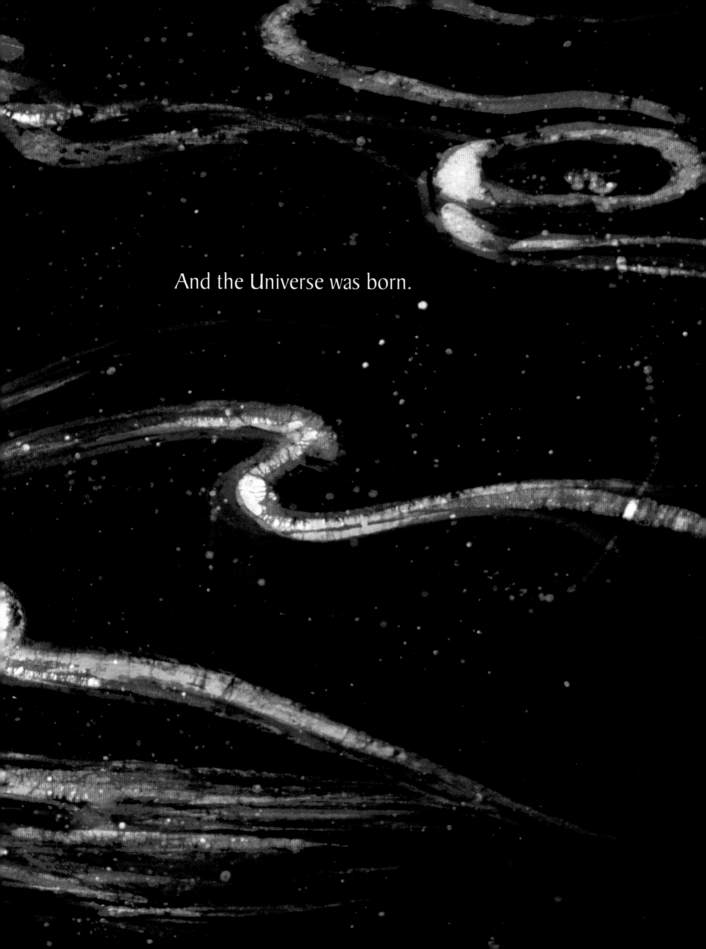

And the Universe was born.

Out fluttered
the galaxies,
like a storm of snowflakes
swirling…

and gathering
into the brightest,
most blindingly beautiful
clouds of stars.

And out of those starclouds
whirled our own star,
the one we call the Sun…

and our Earth

and our Moon…

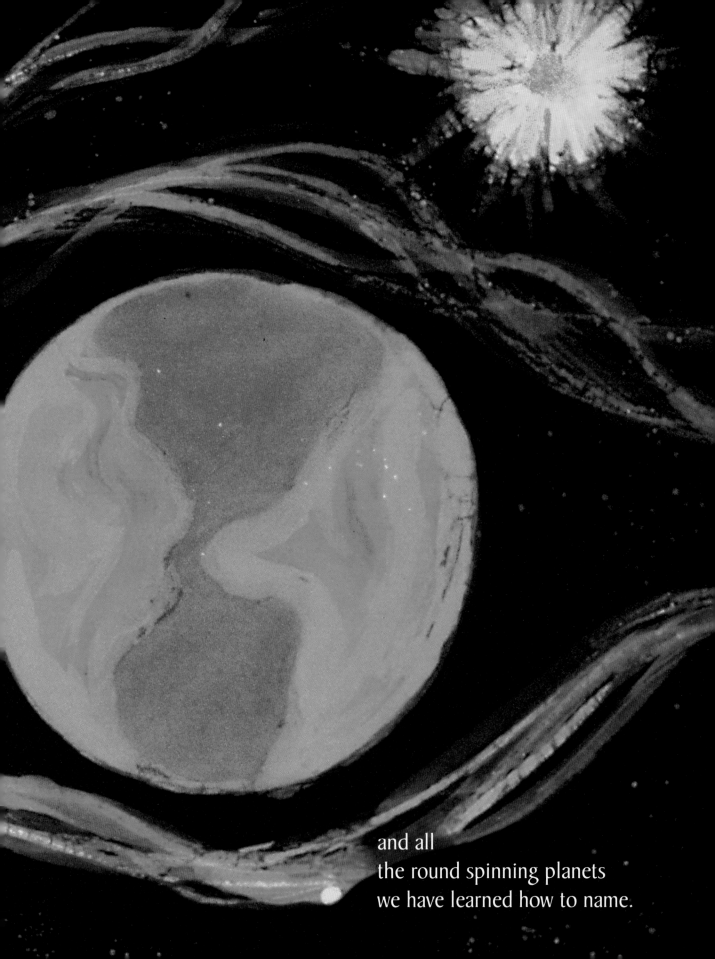

and all
the round spinning planets
we have learned how to name.

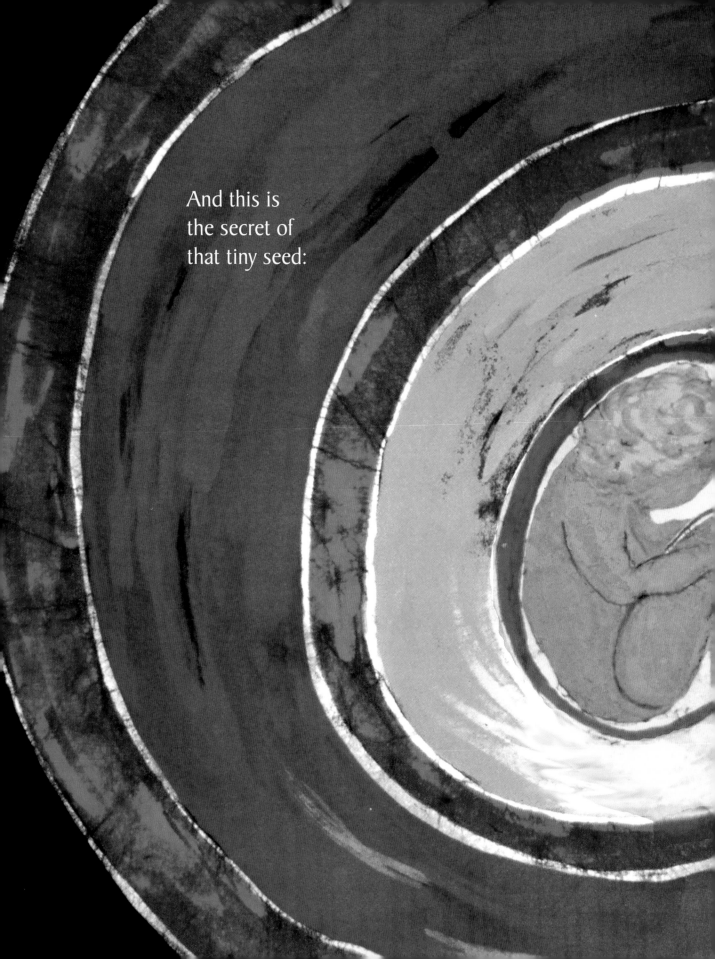

And this is
the secret of
that tiny seed:

You and I
were there
in the very beginning…

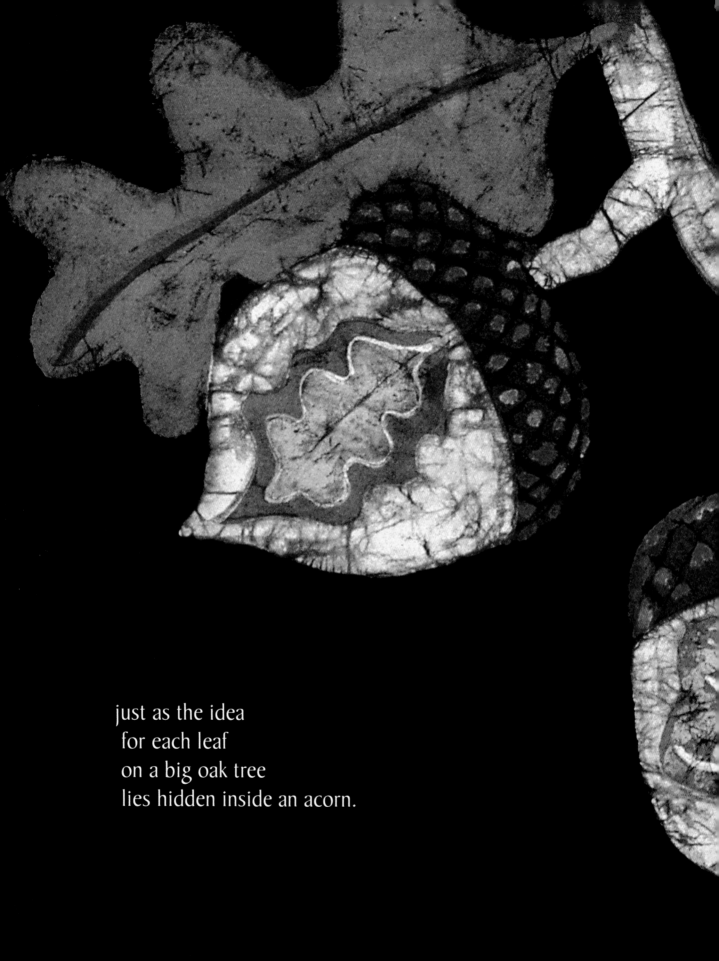

just as the idea
 for each leaf
 on a big oak tree
 lies hidden inside an acorn.

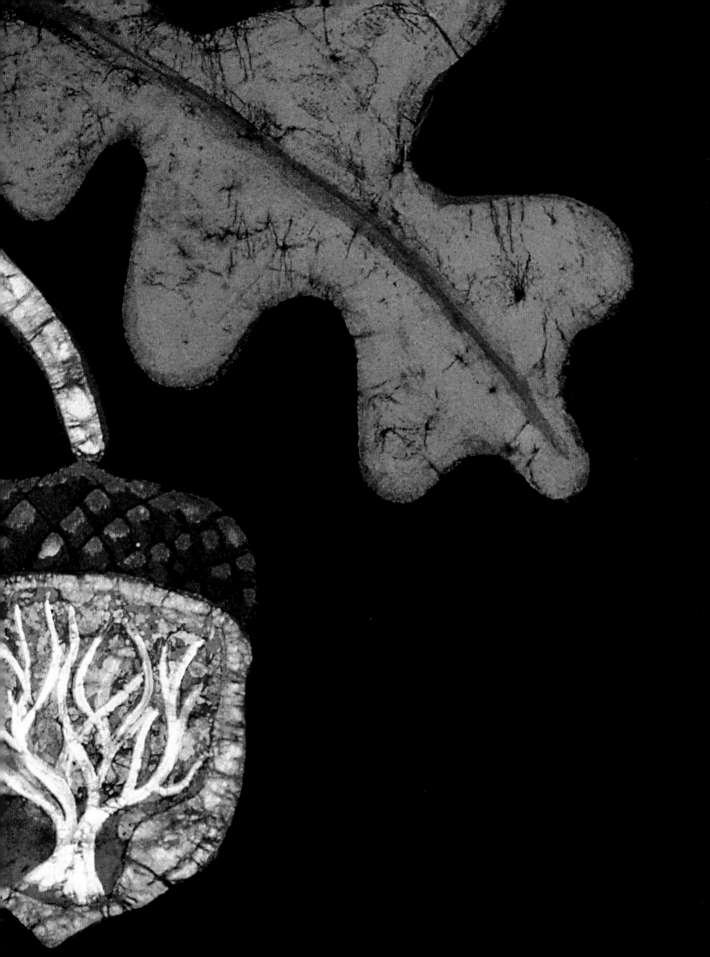

We were there
with all
the stars
and planets,
all the rocks
and oceans,
plants,
and animals,
and people.

Everything
that is now,
ever was,
or ever
will be
was inside
that first
tiny seed.

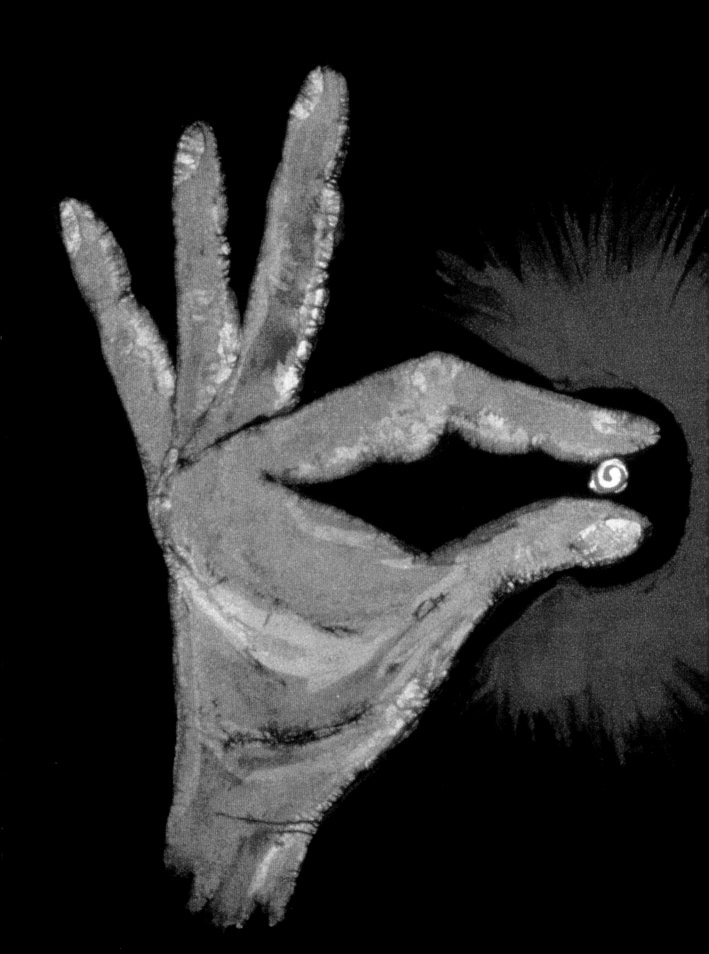

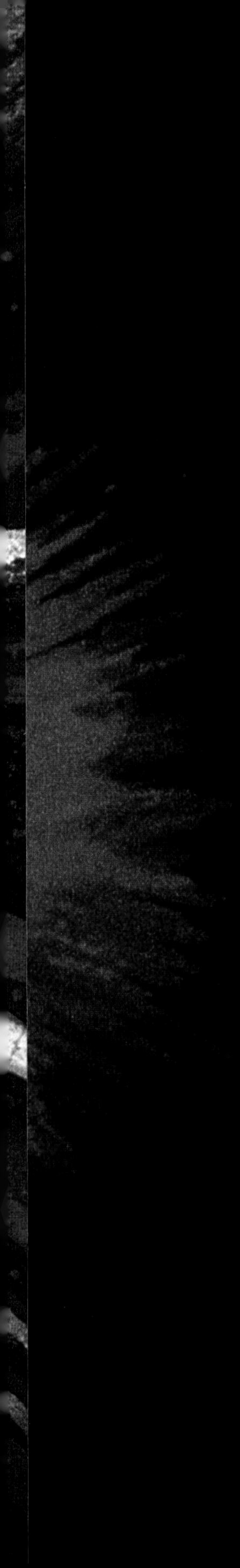

So, whenever
you hold a seed
in your hand
and wonder
what it could become

imagine how you,
and all that is here,
once came from
the tiniest speck
of an Everything Seed

before it sprouted
and grew
long, long ago
in the way-back
beginning of time.

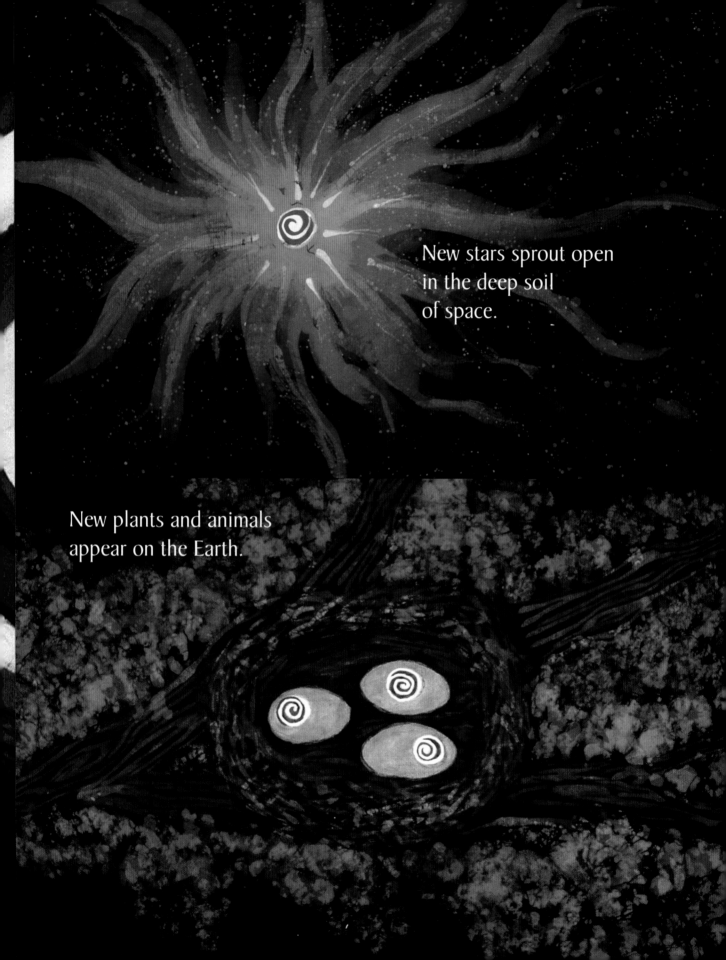

New stars sprout open
in the deep soil
of space.

New plants and animals
appear on the Earth.

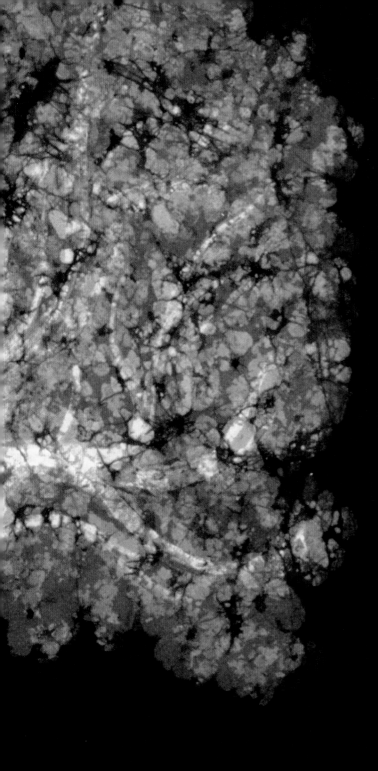

to help us remember.

And new people
are born
every day
with the spark
of that first light
still alive
and burning
deep inside…

waiting…

like
the Everything Seed,
to shine
in ways
that are yet
to be known.

◎ Author's Note ◎

"Every child should be told: you come out of the energy that gave birth to the universe. Its story is your story, its beginnings are your beginnings."

—Mathematical cosmologist Dr. Brian Swimme in "Canticle to the Cosmos."

Stories are born somewhere in the mysterious space between time and imagination. The idea for The Everything Seed had its beginnings in planning a service celebrating the winter solstice.

I looked around in libraries and bookstores for a simple origin myth, one true to the emerging understanding of physics that would use the language of poetry. Then a friend challenged me: "You're a poet. Write your own!" The story was first spoken around an indoor solstice bonfire by a gathering of mythical druids who entered the circle carrying pine boughs and lanterns. It survived to be retold in other settings, evolving over time as it was presented to audiences of many faith traditions, always with the awareness that scientific theories are continually changing.

Instead of an explosion in the militaristic language of the "big bang," this story of the creation uses images of growth that are life-affirming, more expressive of a developing universe. According to mythologist Joseph Campbell and others, the stories we tell ourselves influence how we live. We need our own origin myth, one large enough to activate the religious and cultural imagination of our time. This re-storying of ourselves is necessary for our very survival. Beyond renewed wonder and awe at the unfathomable inventions of nature such as seeds, a central truth of this story is this: everything here is radically related. We are all caught up in an exquisite dynamic of interdependence. To know this at a heart level, to live into it with deep reverence, is my hope for us all.

Carole Martignacco

◎ Illustrator's Note ◎

My goal was to illustrate this new creation myth with creation images from the past. The spiral throughout the book is an ancient symbol of life, growth, and transformation. Inside the Everything Seed is the snake and apple from the Biblical creation story as well as the turtle from Native American creation myths. There are the four elements of fire, water, air, and earth. The plants and animals represent sacred images from a variety of spiritual practices. In this story, these diverse traditions reside together in the Everything Seed, connected at the point of creation. Today, we are still diverse and still connected.

The original artwork for this book is batik. I start by painting designs on white fabric with melted wax. When I immerse the fabric in dye, the waxed places stay white. I repeat this waxing and dyeing process, moving from lightest colors to darkest. Tiny cracks in the wax let in the darker colors and create the crackle lines distinctive to batik. When the wax is removed, the dyed images remain on the fabric. The spiral seed in most pictures was painted on white fabric with fuchsia dye, then waxed over before immersion, allowing a consistent fuchsia color in all the pieces. The picture of the inside of the Everything Seed was painted with dye, but not immersed.

In the batik process, once the fabric is dyed, it IS the new color. Although I can bleach out color, the fabric never truly returns to the pre-dyed hue. Wax that has been applied (or spilled) on fabric is not always possible to remove without ruining the entire piece or starting over. So that spot will BE the color under the wax, like it or not. As batik art unfolds, I can never look back to undo mistakes; I must work with them, knowing they will remain in the final product. And somehow, the batik turns out beautiful in ways that are not always precise or planned. This seems to me very much like life, and therefore a good medium with which to illustrate this story of the unfolding universe.

Joy Troyer

Acknowledgements

Our heartfelt thanks
to family and friends who encouraged Carole to write her own stories,
to Beth Brownfield for believing in this story from the very beginning,
to Suzannah Martin who nudged Joy to take on new artistic challenges,
to Naomi Baer who never wavered in her enthusiasm for this project,
to Mary Samuels who encouraged us to publish the book,
to Cletus Wessels who spread the word about this project,
to United Theological Seminary of the Twin Cities
for its support of spiritually based art and storytelling,
to our friends who reminded us that this is a story for all religions,
and to those many people who provided us
with hope and vision beyond our own.

We are all still unfolding.